Editors: Ann Redpath, Etienne Delessert
Art Director: Rita Marshall
Publisher: George R. Peterson, Jr.

Copyright © 1983 Creative Education, Inc., 123 S. Broad Street,
Mankato, Minnesota 56001, USA. American Edition.
Copyright © 1983 Grasset & Fasquelle, Paris – Editions 24 Heures, Lausanne. French Edition.
International copyrights reserved in all countries.

Library of Congress Catalog Card No.: 83-71173
Icelandic Fairy Tale; Prince Ring
Mankato, MN: Creative Education, Inc.; 32 pages. ISBN: 0-87191-951-6

Printed in Switzerland by Imprimeries Réunies S.A. Lausanne.

PRINCE RING

ICELANDIC FAIRY TALE
illustrated by
HEINZ EDELMANN

CREATIVE EDUCATION INC.

ONCE UPON A TIME

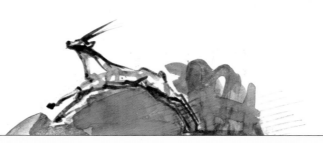

THERE was a King and his Queen living in their kingdom. They had one daughter, who was called Ingiborg, and one son, whose name was Ring. He was less fond of adventures than men of rank usually were in those days, and was not famous for strength or feats of arms. When he was twelve years old, one fine winter day he rode into the forest along with his men to enjoy himself. They went on a long way, until they caught sight of a hind with a gold ring on its horns. The Prince was eager to catch it, if possible, so they gave chase and rode on without stopping until all the horses began to founder beneath them. At last the Prince's horse gave way too, and then there came over them a darkness so black that they could no longer see the hind. By this time they were far away from any house, and thought it was high time to be making their way home again, but they found they had gotten lost now. At first they all kept together, but soon each began to think that he knew the right way best; so they separated, and all went in different directions.

The Prince had gotten lost like the rest, and wandered on for a time until he came to a little clearing in the forest not far from the sea, where he saw a woman sitting on a chair with a big barrel beside her.

The Prince went up to her and saluted her politely, and she received him very graciously. He looked down into the barrel then, and saw lying at the bottom an unusually beautiful gold ring, which pleased him so much that he could not take his eyes off it. The woman saw this, and said that he might have it if he would take the trouble to get it; for which the Prince thanked her, and said it was at least worth trying. So he leaned over into the barrel, which did not seem very deep, and thought he would easily reach the ring. But the more he stretched down after it the deeper grew the barrel. As he was bending down into it the woman suddenly rose up and pushed him in head first, saying that now he could take up his quarters there. Then she fixed the top on the barrel and threw it out into the sea.

The Prince thought himself in a bad plight now, as he felt the barrel floating out from the land and tossing about on the waves. How many days he spent thus he could not tell, but at last he felt that the barrel was knocking against rocks, at which he was a little cheered, thinking it was probably land and not merely a reef in the sea. Being something of a swimmer, he made up his mind to kick the bottom out of the barrel. Having done so, he was able to get on shore, for the rocks by the sea were smooth and level; but overhead there were high cliffs. It seemed difficult to get up these, but he went along the foot of them for a little, till at last he tried to climb up, which at last he did.

Having gotten to the top, he looked round about him and saw that he was on an island, which was covered with forest, with apples growing, and was altogether pleasant as far as the land was concerned.

After he had been there several days, he one day heard a great noise in the forest, which made him terribly afraid, so that he ran to hide himself among the trees. Then he saw a Giant approaching, dragging a sled loaded with wood, and making straight for him, so that all he could do was lie down just where he was. When the Giant came across him, he stood still and looked at the Prince for a little. Then he took him up in his arms and carried him home to his house, and was exceedingly kind to him. He gave him to his wife, saying he had found this child in the wood, and she could have it to help her in the house. The old woman was greatly pleased, and began to care for the Prince with the utmost delight. He stayed there with them, and was very willing and obedient to them in everything, while they grew kinder to him every day.

One day the Giant took him round and showed him all his rooms except the parlor. This made the Prince curious to have a look into it, thinking there must be some very rare treasure there. So one day, when the Giant had gone into the forest, he tried to get into the parlor, and managed to get the door open halfway. Then he saw that some living creature moved inside and ran along the floor towards him and said something, which made him so frightened that he sprang back from the door and shut it again. As soon as the fright began to pass off he tried it again, for he thought it would be interesting to hear what it said; but things went just as before with him. He then got angry with himself and, summoning up all his courage, tried it a third time, and opened the door of the room and stood firm. Then he saw that it was a big Dog, which spoke to him and said:

"Choose me, Prince Ring."

The Prince went away rather afraid, thinking with himself that it was no great treasure after all. But all the same what it had said to him stuck in his mind.

It is not said how long the Prince stayed with the Giant, but one day the latter came to him and said he would now take him over to the mainland, out of the island, for he himself had not a long time to live. He also thanked him for his good service, and told him to choose some one of his possessions, for he would get whatever he wanted. Ring thanked him heartily, and said there was no need to pay him for his services, they were worth so little; but if he did wish to give him anything, he would choose what was in the parlor. The Giant was taken by surprise, and said:

"There, you chose my old woman's right hand, but I must not break my word."

Upon this he went to get the Dog, which came running with signs of great delight; but the Prince was so much afraid of it that it was all he could do to keep from showing his alarm.

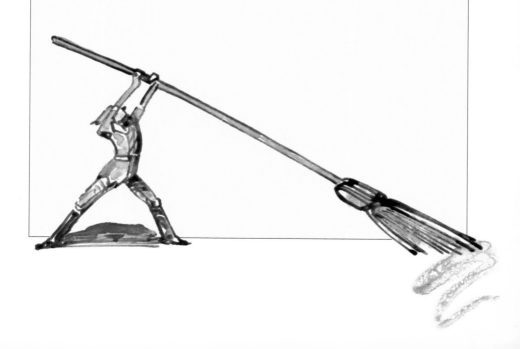

After this the Giant accompanied him down to the sea, where he saw a stone boat which was just big enough to hold the two of them and the Dog. On reaching the mainland the Giant took a friendly farewell of Ring, and told him he might take possession of all that was in the island after he and his wife died, which would happen within two weeks from that time. The Prince thanked him for this and for all his other kindnesses, and the Giant returned home, while Ring went up some distance from the sea; but he did not know what land he had come to, and was afraid to speak to the Dog. After he had walked on in silence for a time, the Dog spoke to him and said:

"You don't seem to have much curiosity, seeing you never ask my name."

The Prince then forced himself to ask, "What is your name?"

"You had best call me Snati-Snati," said the Dog. "Now we are coming to a King's seat, and you must ask the King to keep us all winter, and to give you a little room for both of us."

The Prince now began to be less afraid of the Dog. They came to the King and asked him to keep them all the winter, to which he agreed. When the King's men saw the Dog they began to laugh at it, and make as if they would tease it. But when the Prince saw this he advised them not to do it, or they might have the worst of it. They replied that they didn't care a bit what he thought.

After Ring had been with the King for some days, the King began to think highly of him. The King, however, had a counselor called Red, who became very jealous when he saw how much the King esteemed Ring. One day he talked to him, and said he could not understand why he had so good an opinion of this stranger, who had not yet shown himself superior to other men in anything. The King replied that it was only a short time since he had come there. Red then asked him to send them both to cut down wood next morning, and see which of them could do most work. Snati-Snati heard this and told it to Ring, advising him to ask the King for two axes, so that he might have one in reserve if the first one got broken. Next morning the King asked Ring and Red to go and cut down trees for him, and both agreed. Ring got the two axes, and each went his own way. But when the Prince had gotten out into the wood, Snati took one of the axes and began to hew along with him. In the evening the King came to look over their day's work, as Red had proposed, and found that Ring's woodheap was more than twice as big.

"I suspected," said the King, "that Ring was not quite useless; never have I seen such a day's work."

Ring was now in far greater esteem with the King than before, and Red was all the more discontented. One day he came to the King and said:

"If Ring is such a mighty man, I think you might ask him to kill the wild oxen in the wood here, and flay them the same day, and bring you the horns and the hides in the evening."

"Don't you think that a desperate errand?" said the King, "seeing they are so dangerous, and no one has ever yet ventured to go against them?"

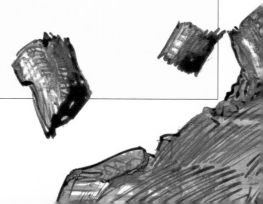

Red answered that he only had one life to lose, and it would be interesting to see how brave he was; besides, the King would have good reason to ennoble him if he overcame them. The King at last allowed himself, though rather unwillingly, to be won over by Red's persistence, and one day asked Ring to go and kill the oxen that were in the wood, and bring their horns and hides to him in the evening. Not knowing how dangerous the oxen were, Ring was quite ready, and went off at once, to the great delight of Red, who was now sure of his death.

As soon as Ring came in sight of the oxen, they came bellowing to meet him; one of them was tremendously big, the other smaller. Ring grew terribly afraid.

"How do you like them?" asked Snati.

"Not well at all," answered the Prince.

"We can do nothing else," said Snati, "than attack them, if it is to go well. You will go against the little one, and I shall take the other."

With this Snati leaped at the big one, and was not long in bringing him down. Meanwhile the Prince went against the other with fear and trembling, and by the time Snati came to help him the ox had nearly gotten him under, but Snati was not slow in helping his master to kill it.

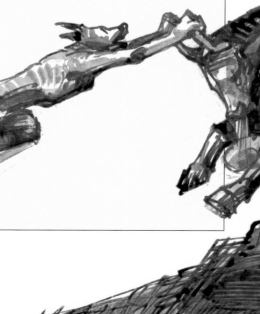

Each of them then began to flay their own ox, but Ring was only half through by the time Snati had finished his. In the evening, after they had finished this task, the Prince thought he was not able to carry all the horns and both the hides, so Snati told him to lay them all on his back until they got to the Palace gate. The Prince agreed, and laid everything on the Dog except the skin of the smaller ox, which he staggered along with himself. At the Palace gate he left everything lying, went before the King, and asked him to come that length with him, and there handed over to him the hides and horns of the oxen. The King was greatly surprised at his valor, and said he knew no one like him, and thanked him heartily for what he had done.

After this the King set Ring next to himself. All esteemed him highly, and held him to be a great hero. And Red could no longer say anything against him, though he grew still more determined to destroy him. One day a good idea came into his head. He came to the King and said he had something to say to him.

"What is that?" asked the King.

Red said that he had just remembered the gold cloak, gold chessboard, and bright gold piece that the King had lost about a year before.

"Don't remind me of them!" said the King.

Red, however, went on to say that, since Ring was such a mighty man who could do everything, it had occurred to him to advise the King to ask him to search for these treasures, and come back with them before Christmas. In return the King should promise him his daughter.

The King replied that he thought it altogether unbecoming to propose such a thing to Ring, seeing that he could not tell him where the things were. But Red pretended not to hear the King's excuses, and went on talking about it until the King gave in to him. One day, a month or so before Christmas, the King spoke to Ring, saying that he wished to ask a great favor of him.

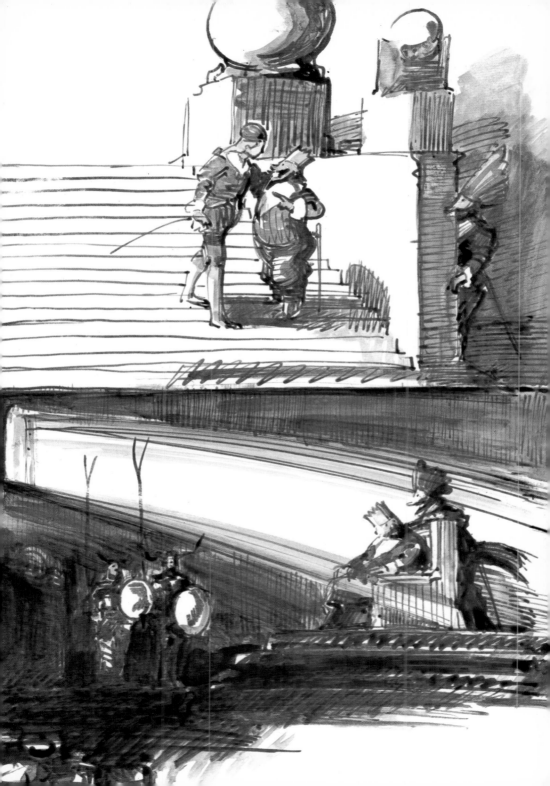

"What is that?" asked Ring.

"It is this," said the King: "that you find for me my gold cloak, my gold chessboard, and my bright gold piece, that were stolen from me about a year ago. If you can bring them to me before Christmas I will give you my daughter in marriage."

"Where am I to look for them, then?" said Ring.

"That you must find out for yourself," said the King. "I don't know."

Ring now left the King, and was very silent, for he saw he was in a great difficulty; but, on the other hand, he thought it was excellent to have such a chance of winning the King's daughter. Snati noticed that his master was at a loss, and said to him that he should not disregard what the King had asked him to do. But he would have to act upon his advice, otherwise he would get into great difficulties. The Prince assented to this, and began to prepare for the journey.

After he had taken leave of the King, and was setting out on the search, Snati said to him, "Now you must, first of all, go about the neighborhood, and gather as much salt as ever you can." The Prince did so, and gathered so much salt that he could hardly carry it; but Snati said, "Throw it on my back," which he accordingly did. The Dog then ran on before the Prince, until they came to the foot of a steep cliff.

"We must go up here," said Snati.

"I don't think that will be child's play," said the Prince.

"Hold fast by my tail," said Snati; and in this way he pulled Ring up on the lowest shelf of the rock. The Prince began to get giddy, but up went Snati onto the second shelf. Ring was nearly swooning by this time, but Snati made a third effort and reached the top of the cliff, where the Prince fell down in a faint. After a little, however, he recovered again, and they went a short distance along a level plain, until they came to a cave.

This was on Christmas Eve. They went up above the cave and found a window in it, through which they looked and saw four trolls lying asleep beside the fire, over which a large porridge-pot was hanging.

"Now you must empty all the salt into the porridge-pot," said Snati.

Ring did so, and soon the trolls woke up. The old hag, who was the most frightful of them all, went first to taste the porridge.

"How comes this?" she said; "the porridge is salt! I got the milk by witchcraft yesterday out of four kingdoms, and now it is salt!"

All the others then came to taste the porridge, and thought it nice, but after they had finished it the old hag grew so thirsty that she could stand it no longer, and asked her daughter to go out and bring her some water from the river than ran near by.

"I won't go," said she, "unless you lend me your bright gold piece."

"Though I should die you shan't have that," said the hag.

"Die, then," said the girl.

"Well, then, take it, you brat," said the old hag, "and be off with you, and make haste with the water."

The girl took the gold and ran out with it, and it was so bright that it shone all over the plain. As soon as she came to the river she lay down to take a drink of the water, but meanwhile the two of them had got down off the roof and thrust her, head first, into the river.

The old hag began now to long for the water, and said that the girl would be running about with the gold piece all over the plain, so she asked her son to go and get her a drop of water.

"I won't go," said he, "unless I get the gold cloak."

"Though I should die you shan't have that," said the hag.

"Die, then," said the son.

"Well, then, take it," said the old hag, "and be off with you, but you must make haste with the water."

He put on the cloak, and when he came outside it shone so bright that he could see to go with it. On reaching the river he went to take a drink like his sister, but at that moment Ring and Snati sprang upon him, took the cloak from him, and threw him into the river.

The old hag could stand the thirst no longer, and asked her husband to go for a drink for her. The brats, she said, were of course running about and playing, just as she had expected they would, little wretches that they were.

"I won't go," said the old troll, "unless you lend me the gold chessboard."

"Though I should die you shan't have that," said the hag.

"I think you may just as well do that," said he, "since you

won't grant me such a little favor."

"Take it, then, you utter disgrace!" said the old hag, "since you are just like those two brats."

The old troll now went out with the gold chessboard, and down to the river, and was about to take a drink, when Ring and Snati came upon him, took the chessboard from him, and threw him into the river. Before they had got back again, however, and up on top of the cave, they saw the poor old fellow's ghost come marching up from the river. Snati immediately sprang upon him, and Ring assisted in the attack, and after a hard struggle they mastered him a second time. When they got back again to the window they saw that the old hag was moving towards the door.

"Now we must go in at once," said Snati, "and try to master her there, for if she once gets out we shall have no chance with her. She is the worst witch that ever lived, and no iron can cut her. One of us must pour boiling porridge out of the pot on her, and the other punch her with a red-hot iron."

In they went then, and no sooner did the hag see them than she said, "So you have come, Prince Ring; you must have seen to my husband and children."

Snati saw that she was about to attack them, and sprang at her with a red-hot iron from the fire, while Ring kept pouring boiling porridge on her without stopping, and in this way they at last killed her. Then they burned the old troll and old hag to ashes, and explored the cave, where they found plenty of gold and treasures. The most valuable of these they carried with them as far as the cliff, and left them there. Then they hastened home to the King with his three treasures, where they arrived late on Christmas night, and Ring handed them over to him.

The King was beside himself with joy, and was astonished at how clever a man Ring was in all kinds of feats, so that he esteemed him still more highly than before, and betrothed his daughter to him; and the feast for this was to last all through Christmastide. Ring thanked the King courteously for this and all his other kindnesses, and as soon as he had finished eating and drinking in the hall went off to sleep in his own room. Snati, asked permission to sleep in the Prince's bed for that night, while the Prince should sleep where the Dog usually lay. Ring said he was welcome to do so, and that he deserved more from him than that. So Snati went up into the Prince's bed, but after a time he came back, and told Ring he could go there himself now, but to take care not to meddle with anything that was in the bed.

Now the story comes back to Red, who came into the hall and showed the King his right arm wanting the hand, and said that now he could see what kind of a man his intended son-in-law was, for he had done this to him without any cause whatever. The King became very angry, and said he would soon find out the truth about it, and if Ring had cut off his hand without good cause he should be hanged; but if it was otherwise, then Red should die. So the King sent for Ring and asked him for what reason he had done this. Snati, however, had just told Ring what had happened during the night, and in reply he asked the King to go with him and he would show him something. The King went with him to his sleeping-room, and saw lying on the bed a man's hand holding a sword.

"This hand," said Ring, "came over the partition during the night, and was about to run me through in my bed, if I had not defended myself."

The King answered that in that case he could not blame him for protecting his own life, and that Red was well worthy of death. So Red was hanged, and Ring married the King's daughter.

The first night that they went to bed together, Snati asked Ring to allow him to lie at their feet, and this Ring allowed him to do. During the night he heard a howling and outcry beside them. He struck a light in a hurry and saw an ugly dog's skin lying near him and a beautiful Prince in the bed. Ring instantly took the skin and burned it, and then shook the Prince, who was lying unconscious, until he woke up. The bridegroom then asked his name; he replied that he was called Ring, and was a King's son. In his youth he had lost his mother, and in her place his father had married a witch, who had laid a spell on him that he should turn into a dog, and never be released from the spell unless a Prince of the same name as himself allowed him to sleep at his feet the first night after his marriage. He added further, "As soon as she knew that you were my namesake she tried to get you destroyed, so that you might not free me from the spell. She was the hind that you and your companions chased; she was the woman that you found in the clearing with the barrel, and the old hag that we just now killed in the cave."

After the feasting was over, the two namesakes, along with other men, went to the cliff and brought all the treasure home to the Palace. Then they went to the island and removed all that was valuable from it. Ring gave to his namesake, whom he had freed from the spell, his sister Ingiborg and his father's kingdom to look after. He himself stayed with his father-in-law the King, and had half the kingdom while the King lived and the whole of it after the King died.

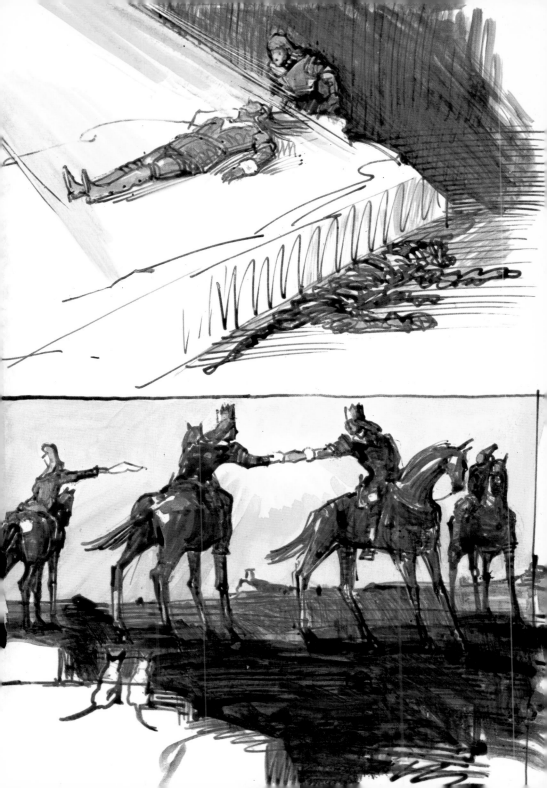